I HAVE TO GO!

A Note from
Robert Munsch

A long, long, LONG time ago when I was in first grade, my class had 60 kids in it!

The teacher didn't read any books and neither did the kids. It was not fun.

Well, here is a book that is fun to read for both you and your grown-ups.

READERS RULE!

Before Reading

High-Frequency Words

Practice reading these high-frequency words in the story:

again   not   these   with

Meet the Characters

Get to know the characters from the story by looking at the pictures and names below:

Andrew

Andrew's father

Andrew's mother

Grandma

All Capital Letters

You might notice in the story that sometimes when Andrew speaks, his words are written in all capital letters. Why do you think these words would be written in only capital letters? Go through the story and read all the lines that are written in all capital letters. Do you notice something about the way these words should be read?

Noun or Not

When a word is a person, place, or thing, it is a noun. All the characters in the story are nouns because they are all people. Take a look at the words below and decide if they are a noun or not.

snowsuit   **car**

bush   **behind**

bathroom   **yell**

There is a **G** sound at the beginning of the word **go**.

Can you make a **G** sound?

Pay close attention to the shape of your mouth as you make the sound. It might be helpful to make this sound while you look in a mirror to see the shape your mouth makes.

Try these different activities to help practice the letter **G** sound.

1. Take a close look around you and try to find three objects that start with the same sound.

2. Think of three other words that also start with the same sound. As an extra challenge, can you think of any words that end with a **G** sound?

3. A simple word that has the **G** sound at the beginning is the word **get**. As you read this word, pay attention to the two other letter sounds in the word.

4. When two words rhyme, they have the same sounds at the end of the word. Take a look at the pictures below and point to any of the words that rhyme with **get**.

pet   **wet**   **fruit**

5. While you read, look out for other **G** sounds at the beginning of a word throughout the story. You can see the sound easily because it will be written in a different color.

I HAVE TO GO!

Story by **Robert Munsch**
Art by **Michael Martchenko**

annick press
toronto • berkeley

To Andrew McIsaac of
Cookstown, Ontario,
and to Andrew Munsch
of Guelph, Ontario

Andrew's mother said,

"Andrew, it's time to go to Grandma

and Grandpa's."

Andrew's father said,

"Andrew, do you have to go pee?"

Andrew said, "NO, NO, NO, NO, NO.

I have decided never to go pee again."

So they drove down the road.

In five minutes Andrew yelled,

"I HAVE TO GO PEE!"

"YIKES," said the father.

"OH NO," said the mother.

Andrew said, "I have to go pee RIGHT NOW!"

So the mother stopped the car and Andrew jumped out and peed behind a bush.

When they got to Grandma and Grandpa's house, Andrew wanted to play in the yard.

Before they put on his snowsuit, the mother and the father and the grandma and the grandpa ALL said, "ANDREW! DO YOU HAVE TO GO PEE?"

Andrew said, "NO, NO, NO, NO, NO."

So they put on Andrew's snowsuit
with a ZIP, BUCKLE BUCKLE, and a
SNAP SNAP SNAP.

Andrew walked out into the backyard,
threw ONE snowball, and yelled,
"I HAVE TO GO PEE."

The father and the mother and

the grandma and the grandpa all

ran outside and got Andrew out

of the snowsuit—

UNSNAP UNSNAP UNSNAP,

UNBUCKLE UNBUCKLE,

UNZIP—

and carried him to the bathroom.

At dinner, Andrew slurped

TWO bowls of soup,

drank THREE glasses of milk,

and ate FOUR scoops of ice cream.

After dinner, the mother and the

father and the grandma and the

grandpa all said, "ANDREW!

DO YOU HAVE TO PEE?"

Andrew said, "NO, NO, NO, NO, NO."

At bedtime,

his mother gave him a kiss—SMERCH!

His father gave him a kiss—SMERCH!

His grandma gave him a kiss—SMERCH!

His grandpa gave him a kiss—SMERCH!

They went downstairs

and waited

and waaaited

and waaaaaaaaaited.

They tiptoed back upstairs.

The father said, "I think he is asleep."

The mother said, "I think he is asleep."

The grandpa said, "I think he is asleep."

The grandma said, "I never had these problems with MY children."

They went downstairs to relax.

And from upstairs, Andrew said,

"GRANDPA! DO YOU HAVE TO GO PEE?"

Grandpa said, "ALL THE TIME!"

So they both went to the bathroom, and then Andrew went to bed and did not have to pee again until morning, not even once.

Retell Activity

Look closely at each picture and describe what is happening in your own words giving as much detail as possible.

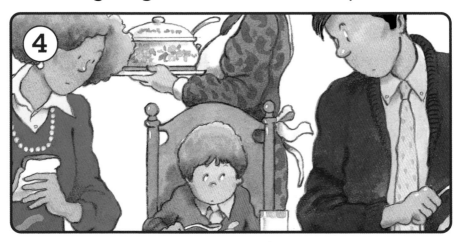

Before you go out on a long trip, what are some important steps you should take before you leave the house?

Take a look at the pictures below and decide if you think they are important or not to do before you leave the house.

Spot the Differences

Look carefully at the two pictures below.
Point to all the differences you can find.

1. Grandma's hair   2. Dad's sweater   3. The painting
4. Grandpa's hair   5. The missing doll

Getting Ready for Reading Tips

- Pick a time during the day when you are most excited to read. This could be when you wake up, after a meal, or right before bedtime.

- Create a special space in your home for reading with some blankets and pillows. The inside of a closet, under a table, or under a bed can make the perfect cozy spot.

- Before you start reading, do a quick look at all the pictures and suggest what the story might be about.

- Can you find the part of the story that repeats?

- Can you add actions like claps, stomps, or jumps to match what is being said to make the words come alive?

- Try to use silly voices for the different characters in the story. Think about changing the volume (e.g., loud, soft), the speed you use to say the words (e.g., fast, super slowly), and how you say the words (e.g., like an animal, like a superhero, like someone older or younger).

- What makes this story silly or funny?

- What part(s) of the story would never happen in real life?

Collect them all!

Adapted from the originals for beginner readers and packed with **Classic Munsch** fun!

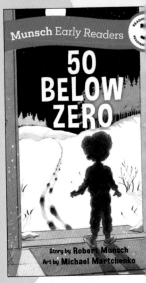

Munsch Early Readers

50 BELOW ZERO

Story by **Robert Munsch**
Art by **Michael Martchenko**

Munsch Early Readers — READING LEVEL **3**

I HAVE TO GO!

Story by **Robert Munsch**
Art by **Michael Martchenko**

Munsch Early Readers

MORTIMER

Story by **Robert Munsch**
Art by **Michael Martchenko**

Munsch Early Readers — READING LEVEL **3**

PIGS

Story by **Robert Munsch**
Art by **Michael Martchenko**

Munsch Early Readers

The Paper Bag Princess

Story by **Robert Munsch**
Art by **Michael Martchenko**

Story by **Robert Munsch**
Art by **Michael Martchenko**

Story by **Robert Munsch**
Art by **Michael Martchenko**

Story by **Robert Munsch**
Art by **Dušan Petričic**

Story by **Robert Munsch**
Art by **Michael Martchenko**

Story by **Robert Munsch**
Art by **Michael Martchenko**

All **Munsch Early Readers**
are level 3, perfect for emergent
readers ready for reading by
themselves—because

READERS RULE!

Robert Munsch, author of such classics as *The Paper Bag Princess* and *Mortimer*, is one of North America's bestselling authors of children's books. His books have sold over 80 million copies worldwide. Born in Pennsylvania, he now lives in Ontario.

Michael Martchenko is the award-winning illustrator of the Classic Munsch series and many other beloved children's books. He was born north of Paris, France, and moved to Canada when he was seven.

© 2022 Bob Munsch Enterprises Ltd. (text)
© 2022 Michael Martchenko (illustrations)

Original publication:
© 1987 Bob Munsch Enterprises Ltd. (text)
© 1987 Michael Martchenko (illustrations)

Designed by Leor Boshi

Thank you to Abby Smart, B.Ed., B.A. (Honors), for her work on the educational exercises and for her expert review.

Annick Press Ltd.
All rights reserved. No part of this work covered by the copyrights hereon may be reproduced or used in any form or by any means—graphic, electronic, or mechanical—without the prior written permission of the publisher.

We acknowledge the support of the Canada Council for the Arts and the Ontario Arts Council, and the participation of the Government of Canada/la participation du gouvernement du Canada for our publishing activities.

ONTARIO ARTS COUNCIL
CONSEIL DES ARTS DE L'ONTARIO
an Ontario government agency
un organisme du gouvernement de l'Ontario

Library and Archives Canada Cataloguing in Publication

Title: I have to go! / story by Robert Munsch ; art by Michael Martchenko.
Names: Munsch, Robert N., 1945- author. | Martchenko, Michael, illustrator.
Description: Series statement: Munsch early readers | Reading level 3: reading with help.
Identifiers: Canadiana (print) 20220170932 | Canadiana (ebook) 20220170940 | ISBN 9781773216515 (hardcover) | ISBN 9781773216416 (softcover) | ISBN 9781773216645 (HTML) | ISBN 9781773216768 (PDF)
Subjects: LCSH: Readers (Primary) | LCGFT: Readers (Publications)
Classification: LCC PE1119.2 .M856 2022 | DDC j428.6/2—dc23

Published in the U.S.A. by Annick Press (U.S.) Ltd.
Distributed in Canada by University of Toronto Press.
Distributed in the U.S.A. by Publishers Group West.

Printed in China

annickpress.com
robertmunsch.com

Also available as an e-book. Please visit annickpress.com/ebooks for more details.